Max and the Magic Word

Colin and Jacqui Hawkins

VIKING KESTREL

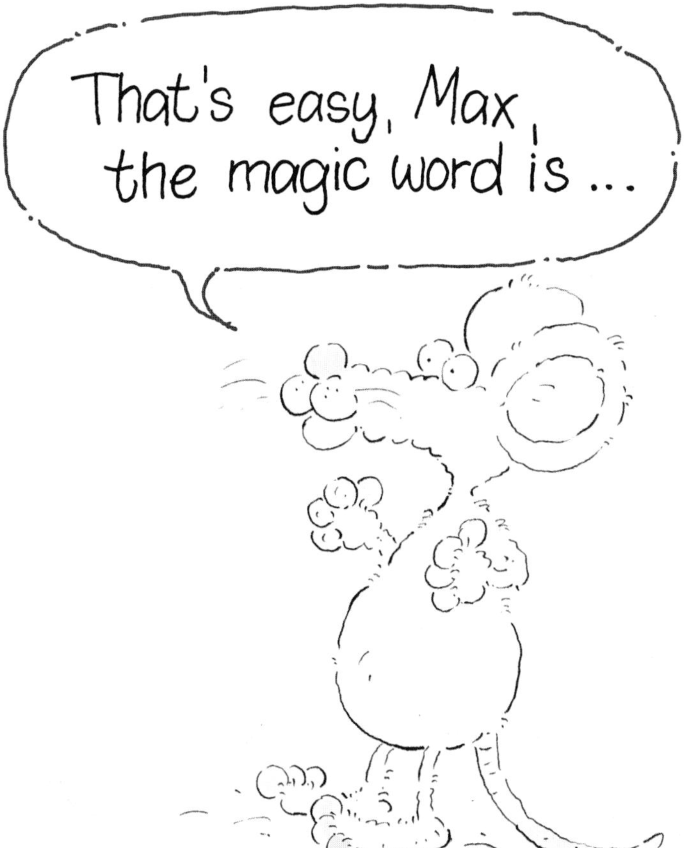
That's easy, Max,
the magic word is ...

Also by Colin and Jacqui Hawkins,
published by Viking Kestrel

My First Book

Jollypops:
Round the Garden
The Elephant
Incy Wincy Spider
This Little Pig

VIKING KESTREL
Penguin Books Ltd, Harmondsworth, Middlesex, England
Viking Penguin Inc., 40 West 23rd Street, New York, New York 10010, U.S.A.
Penguin Books Australia Ltd, Ringwood, Victoria, Australia
Penguin Books Canada Limited, 2801 John Street, Markham, Ontario, Canada L3R 1B4
Penguin Books (N.Z.) Ltd, 182–190 Wairau Road, Auckland 10, New Zealand

First published 1986

Copyright © Colin and Jacqui Hawkins, 1986

British Library Cataloguing in Publication Data available

ISBN 0-670-80853-9

Printed and bound in Great Britain by William Clowes Limited, Beccles and London